'A **raw, powerful, and emot**
violence. This **astonishing** b
needed discussion.'

Kirkus (starred review)

'An **intense** snapshot of the chain reaction caused by pulling a trigger. **Reynolds' concise verses echo like shots** against the white space of the page, their impact resounding.'

Booklist (starred review)

'**Gripping and lightning fast**.'

Bulletin of the Center for Children's Books (starred review)

'A tour de force.'

Publishers Weekly (starred review)

'Jason Reynolds is a **literary genius** who gives voice to a generation. **Powerful, beautiful** and will stay with you long after Will's journey ends. **A masterpiece** from beginning to end.'

Angie Thomas, *The Hate U Give*

'**Fabulistic** in its simplicity . . . It will pair well with *The Hate U Give* . . . Powerful . . . **an important addition to any collection**.'

SLJ (starred review)

'The **best closing line** of a novel this season.'

The Horn Book Magazine (starred review)

FABER & FABER has published children's books since 1929. Some of our very first publications included *Old Possum's Book of Practical Cats* by T. S. Eliot starring the now world-famous Macavity, and *The Iron Man* by Ted Hughes. Our catalogue at the time said that 'it is by reading such books that children learn the difference between the shoddy and the genuine'. We still believe in the power of reading to transform children's lives.

First published in the US by Atheneum Books, an imprint of
Simon & Schuster Children's Publishing Division, in 2017
First published in the UK in 2018
by Faber & Faber Limited
Bloomsbury House,
74–77 Great Russell Street,
London WC1B 3DA

Published by arrangement with Pippin Properties, Inc.
through Rights People, London

Printed in the UK by CPI Group (UK) Ltd, Croydon, CR0 4YY

A CIP record for this book
is available from the British Library

ISBN 978-0-571-33511-4

FSC
www.fsc.org
MIX
Paper from
responsible sources
FSC® C101712

2 4 6 8 10 9 7 5 3 1

LONG WAY DOWN

JASON
REYNOLDS

ILLUSTRATED
BY CHRIS
PRIESTLEY

FABER & FABER

For all the young brothers and sisters
in detention centres around the country,
the ones I've seen, and the ones I haven't.
You are loved.

DON'T NOBODY

believe nothing
these days

which is why I haven't
told nobody the story
I'm about to tell you.

And truth is,
you probably ain't
gon' believe it either
gon' think I'm lying
or I'm losing it,
but I'm telling you,

this story is true.

It happened to me.
Really.

It did.

It *so* did.

MY NAME IS

Will.
William.
William Holloman.

But to my friends
and people
who know me
know me,

just Will.

So call me Will,
because after I tell you
what I'm about to tell you

you'll either
want to be my friend
or not
want to be my friend
at all.

Either way,
you'll know me
know me.

I'M ONLY WILLIAM

to my mother
and my brother, Shawn,
whenever he was trying
to be funny.

Now
I'm wishing I would've
laughed more
at his dumb jokes

because the day
before yesterday,
Shawn was shot

and killed.

I DON'T KNOW YOU,

don't know
your last name,
if you got
brothers
or sisters
or mothers
or fathers
or cousins
       that be like
brothers
and sisters
or aunties
or uncles
       that be like
mothers
and fathers,

but if the blood
inside you is on the inside
of someone else,

you never want to
see it on the outside of
them.

THE SADNESS

is just so hard
to explain.

Imagine waking up
and someone,
a stranger,

got you strapped down,
got pliers shoved
into your mouth,
gripping a tooth

somewhere in the back,
one of the big
important ones,

and rips it out.

Imagine the knocking
in your head,
the pressure pushing
through your ears,
the blood pooling.

But the worst part,
the absolute worst part,

is the constant slipping
of your tongue
into the new empty space,

where you know

a tooth supposed to be

but ain't no more.

IT'S SO HARD TO SAY,

Shawn's
dead.
                Shawn's
dead.
                        Shawn's
dead.

So strange to say.
So sad.

But I guess
not surprising,
which I guess is
even stranger,

and even sadder.

THE DAY BEFORE YESTERDAY

me and my friend Tony
were outside talking about
whether or not we'd get any
taller now that we were fifteen.

When Shawn was fifteen
he grew a foot, maybe a foot
and a half. That's when he gave
me all the clothes he couldn't fit.

Tony kept saying he hoped he grew
because even though he was
the best ballplayer around here
our age, he was also the shortest.

And everybody knows
you can't go all the way when
you're that small unless you can
really jump. Like
                    fly.

AND THEN THERE WERE SHOTS.

Everybody
ran,
ducked,
hid,
tucked
themselves tight.

Did what we've all
been trained to.

Pressed our lips to the
pavement and prayed
the boom, followed by
the buzz of a bullet,
ain't meet us.

AFTER THE SHOTS

me and Tony
waited like we always do,
for the rumble to stop,
before picking our heads up
and poking our heads out

to count the bodies.

This time
there was only one.

Shawn.

I'VE NEVER BEEN

in an   earthquake.
Don't   know if this was
even   close to how they
are,   but the ground
defi   nitely felt like
it o   pened up
and   ate me.

THINGS THAT ALWAYS HAPPEN WHENEVER SOMEONE IS KILLED AROUND HERE

NO. 1: SCREAMING

Not everybody screams.
Usually just

        moms,
        girlfriends,
        daughters.

In this case
it was Leticia,

Shawn's girlfriend,
on her knees kissing
his forehead

between shrieks.

I think she hoped
her voice would
somehow keep him
alive,

would clot the blood.

But I think
she knew

deep down in the
deepest part of
her downness

she was kissing
him goodbye.

AND MY MOM

moaning low,

> *Not my baby.*
> *Not my baby.*
> *Why?*

hanging over my
brother's body
like a dimmed
lamp post.

NO. 2: SIRENS

Lots and lots of sirens,
howling, cutting through
the sounds of the city.

Except the screams.

The screams are always
heard over everything.

Even the sirens.

NO. 3: QUESTIONS

Cops flashed lights in our faces
and we all turned to stone.

Did anybody see anything?

a young officer asked.
He looked honest, like he
ain't never done this before.

You can always tell a newbie.
They always ask questions
like they really expect answers.

Did anybody see anyone?

I ain't seen nothin',

Marcus Andrews, the neighbourhood
know-it-all, said.

Even he knew better than to
know anything.

IN CASE YOU AIN'T KNOW,

gunshots make everybody
deaf and blind especially
when they make somebody

dead.

Best to become invisible
in times like these.
Everybody knows that.

Even Tony flew away.

I'M NOT SURE

if the cops asked me questions.

Maybe.
Maybe not.

Couldn't hear nothing.
Ears filled up with heartbeats
like my head was being held
under water.

Like I was holding my breath.

Maybe I was.
Maybe I was
hoping I could give some
back to Shawn.

Or maybe
somehow

join him.

WHEN BAD THINGS HAPPEN

we can usually look up and see
the moon, big and bright,
shining over us.

That always made me feel better.

Like there's something up there
beaming down on us in the dark.

But the day before yesterday, when
      Shawn
died,

the moon was off.

Somebody told me once a month
the moon blacks out
and becomes new
and the next night be back
to normal.

I'll tell you one thing,
the moon is lucky it's not down here

where nothing
is ever
new.

I STOOD THERE,

mouth clenched
tight enough to grind my
teeth down to dust,

and looked at Shawn
lying there like a piece
of furniture left outside,

like a stained-up couch
draped in a gold chain.
Them fuckers ain't even

snatch it.

RANDOM THOUGHT NO. 1

Blood soaking into a
T-shirt, blue jeans and boots
looks a lot like chocolate syrup
when the glow from the streetlights hit it.

But I know ain't
nothing sweet about blood.
I know it ain't like chocolate syrup

at all.

IN HIS HAND,

a corner-store
plastic bag

white with
red letters

THANK YOU
THANK YOU
THANK YOU
THANK YOU
THANK YOU
THANK YOU
THANK YOU

HAVE A NICE DAY

IN THAT BAG,

special soap
for my mother's

eczema.

I've seen her
scratch until it

bleeds.

Pick at the pus
bubbles and flaky

scales.

Curse the invisible
thing trying to eat

her.

MAYBE THERE'S SOMETHING INVISIBLE

trying
to eat

all of
us as

if we
are beef.

BEEF

gets passed down like name-brand
T-shirts around here. Always too big.
Never ironed out.

Gets inherited like a trunk of fool's
gold or a treasure map leading
to nowhere.

Came knocking on my brother's life,
kicked the damn door down and took
everything except his gold chain.

THEN THE YELLOW TAPE

that says DO NOT CROSS
gets put up, and there's nothing
left to do but go home.

That tape lets people know
that this is a murder scene,
as if we ain't already know that.

The crowd backs its way into
buildings and down blocks
until nothing is left but the tape.

Shawn was zipped into a bag
and rolled away, his blood added
to the pavement galaxy of

bubblegum stars. The tape
framed it like it was art. And the next
day, kids would play mummy with it.

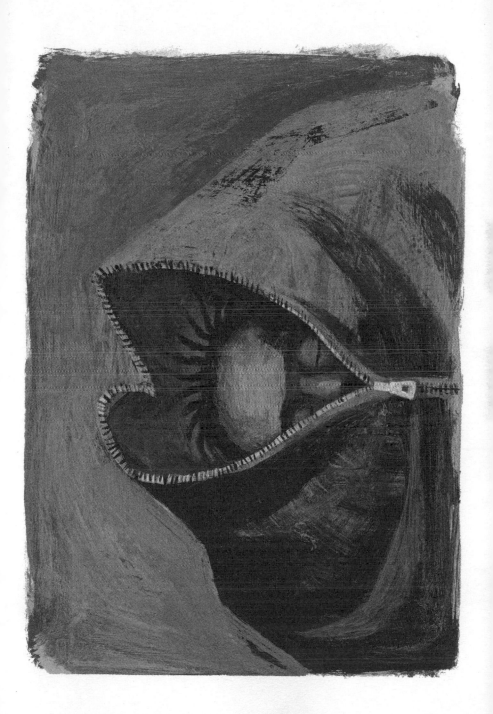

BACK ON THE EIGHTH FLOOR

I locked myself in my room and put
a pillow over my head to muffle
the sound of my mom's mourning.

She sat in the kitchen, sobbing
into her palms, which she peeled
away only to lift glass to mouth.

With each sip came a brief
silence, and with each brief
silence I snuck in a breath.

I FELT LIKE CRYING,

which felt like
another person
trapped behind my face

tiny fists punching
the backs of my eyes
feet kicking
my throat at the spot
where the swallow
starts.

Stay put, I whispered to him.
Stay strong, I whispered to me.

Because crying
is against

The
Rules.

THE RULES

NO. 1: CRYING

Don't.
No matter what.
Don't.

NO. 2: SNITCHING

Don't.
No matter what.
Don't.

NO. 3: REVENGE

If someone you love
gets killed,

find the person
who killed

them and
kill them.

THE INVENTION OF THE RULES

ain't come from my

brother,
his friends,
my dad,
my uncle,
the guys outside,
            the hustlers and shooters,

and definitely not from
me.

ANOTHER THING ABOUT THE RULES

They weren't meant to be broken.
They were meant for the broken

to follow.

OUR BEDROOM: A SQUARE, YELLOWY PAINT

Two beds:
>one to the left of the door,
>one to the right.

Two dressers:
>one in front of the bed to the left of the door,
>one in front of the bed to the right.

In the middle, a small TV.

Shawn's side was the left:
>perfect, almost.

Mine, the right:
>pigsty, mostly.

Shawn's wall had:
>a poster of Tupac,
>a poster of Biggie.

My wall had:
>an anagram I wrote in messed-up scribble
>with a pencil in case Mom made me

erase it:
>SCARE = CARES.

ANAGRAM

is when you take a word
and rearrange the letters
to make another word.

And sometimes the words
are still somehow connected
like: CANOE = OCEAN.

Same letters,
different words,
somehow still make
sense together,

like brothers.

THE MIDDLE DRAWER

was the only thing ever out of place
on Shawn's side of the room,

like a random, jagged tooth
in a perfect mouth,
jammed tight between the
top drawer of shirts
folded into neat rectangles
stacked like project floors,
and the bottom drawer of socks
and underwear.

Off track. Stuck. Forced in at an angle.

Seemed like the middle drawer
was jacked up on purpose
to keep me and Mom out

and Shawn's gun in.

I WON'T PRETEND THAT SHAWN

was the kind of guy
who was home by curfew.

The kind of guy
who called and checked in
about where he was,
who he was with,
what he was doing.

He wasn't.

Not after eighteen,
which was when our mother
took her hands off him,
pressed them together, and

began to pray

that he wouldn't go to jail
that he wouldn't get Leticia pregnant

that he wouldn't   die.

MY MOTHER USED TO SAY,

I know you're young,
gotta get it out,
but just remember, when
you're walking in the night-time,
make sure the night-time
ain't walking into you.

But Shawn
probably had his
headphones on.

Tupac or Biggie.

SO USUALLY

I ended up going to bed
at night, curled up
on my side of the room,
eventually falling asleep staring
at the half-empty bottles of cologne
on top of Shawn's dresser.

And the jacked-up middle drawer.

Alone.

BUT I NEVER TOUCHED NOTHING

because it's no fun
hiding from headlocks
half the night,

which is why I never touched nothing
of his

no more.

IT USED TO BE DIFFERENT.

When I was twelve and he was sixteen
we would talk trash till one of us passed out.

He would tell me about girls, and I would
tell him about pretend girls, who he

pretended were real, too, just to make me
feel good. He would tell me stories about

how the best rappers ever were Biggie and
Tupac, but I always wondered if that was

just because they were dead. People always
love people more when they're dead.

AND WHEN I WAS THIRTEEN

Shawn welcomed me into teenage life
with a spritz of his almost-grown cologne,
said my girlfriend—
       my first girlfriend—
would like it.

But she hated it
so I broke up with her,
because

to me

her nose was
funny acting.

SHAWN THOUGHT THAT

was stupid
and funny
but worthy
of joking me,
calling me

William.
Worthy

of a headlock
that felt like
a hug.

NOW THE COLOGNE

will never drop
lower in the bottles.

And I'll never go to sleep again
believing

that touching them
or anything of his
will lead to an arm
around my neck.

But it feels like an arm
around my neck,
wrenching,
just thinking about how

I'll never go to sleep again
believing him or
believing he

will eventually
come home, because
he won't, and now I guess
I should love him more,

like he's my favourite,

which is hard to do
because he was my only
brother, and

already my favourite.

SUDDENLY

our room
seemed
lopsided.

Cut in half.

Half empty.
Half cold.

Half curious
about that
one drawer

in the middle
of it all.

THE MIDDLE DRAWER CALLED TO ME,

its awkward off-centredness
a sign that what was in it could
and should be used to
set things straight.

I yanked and pulled and
snatched and tugged at
the drawer until it opened
just more than an inch.

Just wide enough for my
fifteen-year-old fingers to
slither in and touch

cold steel.

NICKNAME

A cannon.
A strap.
A piece.
A biscuit.
A burner.
A heater.
A chopper.
A gat.
A hammer.
A tool
  for Rule No. 3.

WHICH BRINGS ME TO CARLSON RIGGS

He was known around
here for being as loud as
police sirens but as
soft as his first name.

PEOPLE SAID RIGGS

talked so much trash because
he was short, but I think it was
because his mom made him take
gymnastics when he was a kid, and
when you wear tights and know how
to do cartwheels it might be a good idea
to also know how to defend yourself.

Or at least talk like you can.

RIGGS AND SHAWN WERE
SO-CALLED FRIENDS, BUT

the best thing he ever did for Shawn
        was teach him how to do a penny drop.

The worst thing he ever did for Shawn
        was shoot him.

A PENNY DROP

is when you hang
upside down on
a monkey bar
and swing
back and forth,
harder and harder,
until just the right
moment, when you
release your legs
and go flying through
the air, hopefully
landing on your feet.

It's all about timing.

If you let your
legs go too early,
you'll land on
your face. If you
let your legs go
too late, you'll land
flat on your back.
So you have to
time it perfectly
to get it right.
Shawn taught me

how to time it perfectly.

If you could do a
penny drop or a
backflip (no cartwheels)
you were the king.
Shawn could do
both so he was the
king around here to
me and Tony and
all our friends.
But he made sure
I was the prince.

In case you ain't know.

REASONS I THOUGHT (KNEW) RIGGS KILLED SHAWN

NO. 1: TURF

Riggs moved to a
different part of the hood
where the Dark Suns
hang and bang and be wild.

He wanted to join so he
wouldn't be looked at like
all bark no more,
and instead could have

a backbone built for him
by the bite of his block boys
who wait for anyone to cross
the line into their territory,

which happens to be nine
blocks from our building,
and in the same neighbourhood
as the corner store

that sells that special soap
my mother sent Shawn
out to get for her the
day before yesterday.

NO. 1.1: SURVIVAL TACTICS (made plain)

Get
down
with
some
body

or

get
beat
down
by
some
body.

NO. 2: CRIME SHOWS

I grew up watching crime
shows with my mother.

Always knew who the killer
was way before the cops.

It's like a gift. Anagrams,
and solving murder cases.

NO. 3: . . . .

Had to be.

I HAD NEVER HELD A GUN.

Never even
touched one.

Heavier than
I expected,

like holding
a newborn

except I
knew the

cry would
be much

much much
much louder.

A NOISE FROM THE HALLWAY

My mother,
stumbling to the bathroom,
her sobs leading the way.

I quickly slapped
the switch on the wall, dropping
the room into darkness, dropping
myself into bed, pushing
the pistol under my pillow
like a lost tooth.

SLEEP

ran from me
for what seemed
like forever,

hid from me
like I used to hide
from Shawn

before finally
peeking out from
behind pain.

I WOKE UP

in the morning
and tried to remember
if I dreamed about
anything.

I don't think I did,
so I pretended that
I dreamed about
Shawn.

It made me feel better
about going to sleep
the night he was
murdered.

BUT I ALSO FELT GUILTY

for waking up,
for breathing in,

for stretching,
yawning, and
reaching

under
the pillow.

I WRAPPED MY FINGERS

around the grip, placing
them over Shawn's
prints like little
brother holding big
brother's hand again,

walking me to the store,
teaching me how to
do a penny drop.

If you let go too early
you'll land on your face.
If you let go too late
you'll land on your back.
To land on your feet,
you gotta time it just right.

IN THE BATHROOM

in the mirror
my face sagged,
like sadness
was trying to pull
the skin off.

Zombie.

I had slept
in my clothes,
the stench of
death and sweat
trapped in the
cotton like
fish grease.
I looked and
felt like

shit.

And so what.

I STUCK THE CANNON

in the waistband in the
back of my jeans, the
handle sticking out like a
                    steel tail.

I covered it with
my too-big T-shirt,
the name-brand
hand-me-down
                    from Shawn.

THE PLAN

was to wait for Riggs
in front of his building.

Me and Shawn were
always over his house
before Riggs joined the gang,

and since then, Shawn had been
up that way a bunch of times
to get Mom's special soap.

I figured it would be safest
if I went in the morning. If I
timed it right, none of his crew

would be out yet. No one
would ever suspect me. I'd hit
his buzzer, get him to come down

and open the door. Then I'd pull my
shirt over my mouth and nose

and do it.

IN THE KITCHEN

the sun burst through the
window, bathing my mother,
who slept slumped at the
table, her head resting in the
nest of her red, swollen arms.

She'd probably been scratching
all night, maybe trying to scratch
the guilt away. I wanted to
wake her and tell her that it
wasn't her fault, but I didn't.

Instead, with the pistol heavy
on my back, I stepped lightly
over the creaky parts of the
floor, trying not to wake her
and lie about where I was going.

And break her heart even more.

THE YELLOW LIGHT

that lined the hallway
buzzed like the lightning
bugs me and Shawn
used to catch when
we were kids.

We scooped them
into washed-out mayo
jars four or five
at a time.

Shawn would twist
the lid tight, and the
two of us would sit
on a bench and watch
them fly around,
bumping into each other,
trapped, until
one by one
their lights went out.

AT THE ELEVATOR

Back already sore.
Uncomfortable.
Gun strapped
like a brick
rubbing my skin
raw with each step.

Seemed like time
stood still as I
reached out and
pushed the button.

White light
surrounded the
black arrow.

DOWN
DOWN
DOWN DOWN DOWN
DOWN DOWN
DOWN

.

THERE'S A STRANGE THING

that happens
in the elevator.
In any elevator.

Every time
somebody gets
in, they check
to see if the button
for the floor they're
going to is lit,
and if it isn't,
they push it,
then face
the door.

That's it.

They don't
speak to the
people already
in the elevator,
and the
people already
in the elevator
don't speak to
the newcomer.

Those are
elevator rules,
I guess.

No talking.
No looking.
Stand still,
stare at the door,
and wait.

09:08:02 a.m.

A GUY GOT ON,

definitely older than me,
but not old.
Medium-brown skin.
Slim. Low haircut,
part on the side.

No hair on his face, none at all.
Not even a moustache.

Gold links dangling
around his neck
like magic rope.

Checked to
make sure
the *L* button was lit.

Going down too.

L STOOD FOR "LOSER"

when we were kids,
so Shawn and I would
stand in an empty elevator
and wait for someone to get on
and push *L*. And when they did, we
would giggle because they were the
loser and me and Shawn were winners
on a funny and victorious ride down to the
lobby. I thought about this when the man with
the gold chains got on and checked to see if the
L button was already glowing. I wondered if he knew
that in me and Shawn's world, I'd already chosen to be

a loser.

IT'S UNCOMFORTABLE

when you
feel like
someone
is looking
at you but
only when
you not
looking.

I'VE SEEN GIRLS

waiting at the bus stop
make men pitiful pieces
of putty, curling backwards,
stretching and straining
every muscle just to get
a glimpse of what Shawn
and a lot of men
around here call

the world.

But there were no women
in this elevator, so there
were no worlds to be
checkin' for.

But he kept checkin'
anyway,
not knowing that
if he kept checkin'
anyway
he'd get

a world

of trouble.

09:08:04 a.m.

DO I KNOW YOU?

I asked,
irritated,
freaked out.

The man smiled,
adjusted the chains
around his neck.

Looked me
straight in the eyes,
dead in the face.

You don't recognise me?

he asked,
his voice
deep,
familiar.

I looked harder.
Squinted, trying to
place the face.

Nah. Not really,

I said.

He smiled wide.

A jagged mouth,
sharp and sharklike.

Then turned around
so that I could see the
back of his T-shirt.

A silk-screened photo.
Him, squatting low.
Middle fingers in the air.
And a smile made
of triangles.

RIP BUCK YOU'LL BE MISSED 4EVA

MY STOMACH JUMPED

into my chest
or my chest fell
into my stomach.

Or both.
I knew him.

Buck?

I stumbled

backwards.
Couldn't be.
Couldn't be.

Ain't that what it say?

he said,

facing me.
Couldn't be.
Couldn't be.

But I thought . . .

I stuttered.

I thought . . . I thought . . .

You thought I was dead,

he said,

straight up.
Straight up.

I RUBBED MY EYES

over and over and
over and over again,

trippin'.

Never smoked
or nothing like that.

Don't know high life.
Don't know bad trips.
Don't no dead man

supposed to be
talking to me, though.

YEAH

I did,

I said,
hoping he would
come back with
I'm not dead or *I
faked my death*
or

something
like that.

Or maybe
I'd wake up, sit
straight up
in bed,
the gun still tucked
under my pillow,
my mother still asleep
at the kitchen table.

A dream.

Buck looked at me,
noticing my panic,
softly said,

I am.

I DID ALL THE WAKE-UP TRICKS.

Pinched the meat
in my armpit,
slapped myself
in the face,
even tried to
blink myself
awake.

Blink,
blink,
blink,

but

       Buck.

I KNOW WHAT YOU THINKIN'.

That I was scared
~~of~~
to death.

BUT NO NEED TO BE AFRAID.

I had known Buck
since I was a kid
the only big brother
Shawn had ever had.

Shawn knew Buck
better than I did,
knew Buck longer than
we'd known our dad.

I TAKE IT BACK.

I *was* scared.

What if he had come
to get me,
to take me
with him?

What if he had come
to catch
my breath?

ANAGRAM NO. 1

ALIVE = A VEIL

09:08:05 a.m.

CATCHING MY BREATH, I ASKED,

So why you here?

> I wiped
> the corners
> of my mouth, thought,
>
> *Please don't say*
> *you've come to*
> *take me.*
>
> *Please don't say*
> *I'm dead.*
>
> *Please.*
>
> > *Actually,*
>
> he said,
> doing the bus-stop
> lean back again,
>
> > *I came to check*
> > *on my gun.*

MY RESPONSE

...

Then, finally,
in an almost-whisper, he added,

Your tail is showing.

I PUT MY HAND BEHIND MY BACK,

felt the imprint
of the piece, like
another piece
of me,

an extra vertebra,
some more
backbone.

THOUGHT ABOUT MOVING IT

to the front,

but Shawn used to always say
dogs,
even snarling ones,
tuck their tails between their legs,

a sign of fear.
A signal of

bluff.

I REMEMBER

when I gave
that thing to Shawn,

Buck said,

He was around your age.
Told him he could hold it for me.
Taught him how to use it too.
Taught him The Rules.
Made him promise to put it
somewhere you couldn't get it.

and I replied
with as much
tough in
my voice as
I could.

But I got it.

AND I'M GLAD I FOUND IT,

because I'm gonna need it,

    I explained.

Shawn's dead now.

        No need to tiptoe around it.
        Plus, I figured Buck already knew.
        Figured dead know dead stuff.
        Damn.
        (Dumb thing to think.)

Happened last night.
Followed him from the store.
Caught him slippin',
gave him two to the chest
right outside our building,

        I said,
        anger sour in the back
        of my throat.

But I know it was the
Dark Suns. Riggs and
them. Had to be.

        Buck folded his arms.

I see,

he said,
shaking his head,
his mouth fading
into frown.

So what you 'bout to do?

My eyes turned
to razor blades.

*I'm about to do what
I gotta do. What you
woulda done.*

I squared.

Follow The Rules.

09:08:08 a.m.

THE ELEVATOR RUMBLED

and vibrated
and knocked
around like the middle drawer,
like something was off track.

Scared the hell outta me.

What's taking
this stupid
thing so long?

I asked,
pounding the door
as hard
as my heart was
pounding inside me.

*This rickety thing
has always moved slow,*

Buck said,
grinning.

*Yeah, but this
is ridiculous,*

I replied,
palms wetting.

Might as well relax,

Buck said.

*It's a long
way
down.*

MAYBE HE DIDN'T HEAR ME

or didn't take me seriously.

Old people always do that.
Always try to act like what I'm saying ain't true.
Always try to act like I'm not forreal.

But I was forreal.

> *So* forreal.

RELAX?!

I snapped.

Relax?
I ain't got time to relax!
I got work to do.
A job to do.
Business to handle,

I said,
feeling myself,
my macho
between

my shaky legs,
masking
my jumpy heart.

BUCK LAUGHED, AND

laughter,

when it's loud
and heavy
and aimed
at you,

I think
can feel just
as bad as
a bullet's

bang.

YOU GOT WORK TO DO?

A job to do?

Buck teased,
wiping laugh-tears
from his eyes.

Right, right. You gon' follow
The Rules, huh?

Yeah, that's right,

I said,
opening my stance
to let him know this
wasn't a game,
that I was forreal.

Buck pressed
his finger to my chest
like he was pushing an
elevator button.
The L button.

But you ain't
got it in you, Will,

he said,
cocky.

Your brother did, but you—
you don't.

HE ASKED ME

if I had even checked
to see if the gun was
loaded.

I hadn't.

And now almost shot
myself trying
to figure out
how to.

GIVE IT TO ME

before
you hurt yourself.

Buck clicked something.

The clip slid from the grip
like a metal candy bar.

Fourteen slugs.
One in the hole.
Fifteen total,

he said,
slamming
the clip back in.

How many
should there be?

I asked.

Sixteen.
But, whatever.

09:08:11 a.m.

HE HELD THE GUN OUT.

I grabbed it,
but Buck wouldn't let go.

I yanked and yanked,
pulled and pulled,

but he

resisted and resisted,
laughed and laughed,

bucked and bucked.

BUCK FINALLY LET GO

and I stumbled into the corner,
slamming against the wall

like a clown.

> *You don't got it in you,*

he repeated
over and over again
under his un-breath
while sliding a pack
of cigarettes from
his pocket.

Tossed one in his mouth,
struck a match that sounded
like a finger snap.

Then the elevator came to a stop.

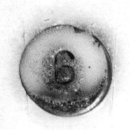

I HAD HALF A SECOND

to

get a grip,
grab the grip,
tuck the gun,
turn around,
ignore Buck,
catch my breath,
stand up straight,
act normal
act natural
act like
the only rules
that matter
are the ones
for the elevator.

A GIRL STEPPED IN.

Stood beside me.
Around my age.
Fine as heaven.
Flower dress.
Low heels.
Light make-up,
        lip gloss,
        cheek stuff.
Perfume,
        sweet,
        fresh,
        cutting
        through the cigarette smoke.

SHE CHECKED TO MAKE SURE

L was lit.
And I was

walking my eyes
up her legs,
the ruffle and fold
of her flower
dress, her
arms, her
neck, her
cheek, her
hair.

Then
the bus-stop
lean back
to get a glimpse

of the world.

But the metal barrel
dug into my back,
making me wince,
making me obvious

and wack.

I DIDN'T KNOW

> *smoking*
> *was allowed*
> *in elevators,*

she said,
her small talk smacking
with sarcasm.
But I was too shook
to notice.

You . . . can see that?

I replied
all goofy,
my game no good
around ghosts.

I wondered if she
thought it was me
lighting up
before she
got on

since she couldn't see
Buck in the corner
puffing out,
making faces like,
Get on
with it.

Uh . . . of course.
It's everywhere,

she said,
pinching
back a cough.

She fanned smoke
from her face,
and thumbed to Buck,
who shook his head and
blew vanishing halos.

She could see him.
She could see him?
She could see him!

Then
she turned to me
and added,

> *I didn't know*
> *guns*
> *were allowed*
> *in elevators either.*

SHE COULD SEE

Buck?
But how?
I thought he was

only my ghost,
only my grand
imagination.

But
when she
could see him,
could smell his funky
cigarette,
I knew for a fact
this was real.

AT THIS POINT

you probably
already don't
believe me
or think I'm nuts.

And maybe I am.

But I swear
this is all
true.

Swear.

I JOINED IN,

fanning the smoke,
shaking her comment
about the gun,
looking at Buck
all crazy.

But he ain't care.

Just leaned back and
took another pull on the cig,
burning but not burning down.

Still long.
Fire.
Smoke.

But no ash.

SHE BRUSHED HER HAND AGAINST MINE

to get my attention,
which on any other
occasion would've
been the perfect
open for me to flirt
or at least try to do
my best impression of Shawn,

which was
his best impression of Buck.

BUT THERE WAS A GHOST
IN THE ELEVATOR

so,
no-
go.

PLUS

**it's hard to think about
kissing and killing
at the same time.**

SHE ASKED,

*What you need
it for anyway?*

And when I
looked confused
(pretended to
look confused),

she ticked
tongue to teeth
and clarified,

The gun.

09:08:15 a.m.

THE NEXT EXCHANGE WAS A SIMPLE ONE.

I don't mean no harm,
but that ain't something
you just ask someone
you don't even know,

I said,
still trying to
play cool.

The girl nodded,
replied,

You're right.
So right.

BUT THEN

she put her hand on my shoulder,
her perfume floating from her wrist
to just under my nostrils, said,

> *But*
> *I do*
> *know*
> *you,*
>
> *Will.*

I WON'T FRONT.

I was a little excited.

I know I just said flirting
in an elevator with
a ghost on it was a
no-
go,

but we wouldn't be
in this elevator forever.

And Shawn always said
if a girl says she knows you
but you ain't never met her
then she's been
watching you.
Clockin' you.
Checkin' you.

Buck probably taught him that.
I hoped it was true.

FROM WHERE?

is what I came with next,
loading up my flirts.

Where you know me from?

The girl smiled.
With her eyes.

From the playground,

she said.

Monkey bars.

VERY FUNNY,

I said,
picking up on
her trying to play me.

I ain't no monkey.

I never said you were,

she replied.

I'm being serious.

Well, then you got the
wrong guy because I'm too
old to be hanging
at playgrounds.

Yeah, but I knew you
when you weren't.

SHE OPENED HER PURSE,

dug around,
pulled out a wallet,
unfolded it,
turned it towards
me to flash a photo
like white people
in movies when they

want to show off their kids.

But I wasn't trying to see no kids.
But there they were.

There we were.

ME AND MY FRIEND DANI

as kids.
Eight
years old.

No-knee'd jeans and
hand-me-down T-shirt
from Shawn.

Flower dress,
shorts underneath
for Dani,
who hung from a monkey bar
tongue hanging from her mouth
like pink candy.

The sun shining in my eyes.
The sunshine in hers.

09:08:18 a.m.

YOU REMEMBER THIS?

the girl asked,
folding
snapping
the wallet shut.

Of course,

I said,
wondering how she
knew Dani.

*It was one of the best
and worst days of my life.*

You remember, on this day,

she paused,
cocking her
head to the side,
hands on hips,
butterflied arms,
and continued,

I kissed you?

MY EYES GOT BIG.

Dani?

> This was Dani. Dani.
> Standing in front of me.
>
> The flower dress
> the same.
>
> Her face
> eight years older than
> eight years old
> but still
>
> the same.

YEAH, I REMEMBER.

I remember.
I remember that.
I remember this.
And then . . .

I got hung up.

And then . . .

Gunshots,

she said.

Gunshots.

GUNSHOTS

like firecrackers
coming from everywhere.

Dani said her body burned
and all she wanted to do was
jump outside of herself,
swing to somewhere else

like we pretended to do
on monkey bars.

AND NOW I WANNA THROW UP,

Buck baited.

He *heh-heh-heh*'d,
the cigarette dangling,
bouncing with each word
like a fishing pole
with fish on bait,
with hook through head.

I TOLD DANI

how I remember
Shawn screaming for us to
get down.

How he lay on top of us,
covering us, smashing us
into the dirt.

I told her how I remember
staring at her the whole
time.

Her eyes wide, the brightness
dimming. Her mouth, open.
Bubble gum

and blood.

I SWEAR SOMETIMES

it feels like God
be flashing photos
of his children,
awkward,
amazing,

tucked in his wallet
for the world
to see.

But the world
don't wanna see
no kids,

and God ain't
no pushy parent
so he just folds
and snaps
us shut.

WHEN THEY SAID

you were gone,
I cried all night,

       I confessed.

And the next morning,
over hard-boiled eggs
and sugar cereal,
Shawn taught me
Rule Number One—

no crying.

THE WAY I FELT

when Dani was killed
was a first.

Never felt nothing like it.

I stood in the shower
the next morning
after Shawn taught me
the first rule,
            no crying,
feeling like
I wanted to scratch
my skin off scratch
my eyes out punch
through something,
            a wall,
            a face,
            anything,
so something else
could have
a hole.

ANAGRAM NO. 2

FEEL = FLEE

IT'S COOL

to see you, Dani,

      I said,
      feeling funny
      but meaning
      every word.

      She grew up
      gorgeous.

      At least
      she would've.

            Good to see
            you too, Will.

      She grinned.

            But you still haven't
            answered my question.

WHAT YOU NEED

a gun for?

09:08:20 a.m.

MY FACE

**tightened
hardened.**

They killed Shawn last night.

             Who killed Shawn?

Shouldn't you already know?

             Just tell me who killed him, Will.

*The Dark Suns. You remember
Riggs, used to live around here?
I think it was him. Had to be?*

     **Had
to
be.**

DANI WAS KILLED

before she ever learned
The Rules.

So I explained them to
her so she wouldn't think
less of me for following
them

like I was just another
block boy on one
looking to off one.

So that she knew I had
purpose

and that this was about
family

and had I known
The Rules when we
were kids I would've
done the same thing

for her.

THEN DANI ASKED,

What
if
you

miss?

BUT

I won't,

      I said.

            But what if you do?

      she asked.

I won't,

      I said.

            But, how you know?

      she asked.

I just know,

      I said.

            But, you ever even shot a gun?

      she asked.

Don't matter,

      I said.

      Don't matter.

DANI WAS DISAPPOINTED.

Slapped her
hands to her face,
tried to wipe
away worry.

But she couldn't.
And I couldn't
expect her to.

I LOOKED BACK AT BUCK

for a bailout,
some help,
something,
but he said
nothing.

Just slid the
cigarettes
from his pocket
and extended it
to Dani.

BUCK OFFERED,

Smoke?

> I guess this
> was his way
> of diffusing the
> situation.

> > *Thank you,*

> Dani said,
> wiggling one
> from the box.

You smoke?

> I asked.

> > *You shoot?*

> she shot back,
> slipping it between
> shiny lips,
> leaning forwards
> for the light.

> Buck struck
> a match.

> And again
> the elevator came to a stop.

THE ELEVATOR,

a smoke box,
grey and thick.

Buck and Dani
puffed and blew
everlasting cigs.

Thought when the
doors opened the
smoke would rush out.

But instead it
became a still cloud
trapped in a steel cube.

CIGARETTE SMOKE

ain't supposed to be
no wool blanket,
ain't supposed to be
no blizzard, no
snowy TV.

Smoke   like spirit
can be thick but
ain't supposed to be
nothing solid
enough to hold me.

I FANNED AND COUGHED,

expecting whoever was waiting
to wait for the next one.

Who wants to get in an elevator
full of smoke?

But what if it wasn't really
full of smoke?

Still,
who wants to get in an elevator
with a kid buggin'?

Swatting and choking on
the invisible thick.

They'd probably think
what you probably think
right now.

I TOOK A STEP BACK

to make room
for the silhouette to
move through the fog,

to step in.

Dani and Buck
stood behind me,
close enough to feel

but I felt no breath.

TWO LARGE HANDS,

the largest I'd ever seen,
came through the cloud

hard and fast,

snatched fistfuls of my shirt,
yoking me by the neck,
holding me there until
the elevator door closed.

Could barely breathe
already and could breathe
less and could see nothing
behind this blanket

of grey.

THEN IN ONE SWIFT MOTION

the hands released me and
slapped me into a headlock,

the kind that Shawn used to
put me in, the kind that all little

brothers hate.

I COULD HEAR LAUGHING

like being held under water
by playful waves
crashing down on my head
laughing laughing
laughing me under.

How do you tell water
ain't nothing funny
about drowning?

WHEN I WAS FINALLY LET UP

I looked

for Buck,
for Dani,
for help.

They moved
to the corner,
chuckling,
blurry,
puffing

away.

WHAT THE HELL?

I
yelped,

one hand on my neck,
one hand on my tucked

untucked
tail.

WHAT YOU REACHIN' FOR

and why you reachin' for it?

the asshole
who tried to mash
the apple in my neck
into sauce
taunted.

Nephew

Nephew   *Nephew*

Nephew!   *Nephew,*

he chanted,

*After all this time
you ain't learned to
fight back yet?*

THERE ARE

so many pictures
of Uncle Mark in
our house.

Hanging on the wall,
hanging on the block, posing
with my father, his shorter
younger brother.

Dressed blade sharp.
Suits, jewellery.
Cigarette tucked
behind ear.
Camera ready.

Fly.
Like Shawn.
Foreshadowing the flash.

UNCLE MARK?

I let my hand fall
to my side
swallowed hard.

Am I going insane?

         Come here, kid,

Uncle Mark said.

         Lemme look at ya.

I stepped closer.

Taller than me.
Taller than everyone.
Six foot four,
Six foot five.
(Six feet deep.)

Rested his hands
on my shoulders,
the weight of him
bending me
at the knees.

         Look like your damn daddy,

he said.

         Just like him.

MY MOTHER TOLD ME TWO STORIES
ABOUT UNCLE MARK.

NO. 1

He videotaped everything
with a camera his mother,
my grandmother, bought him
for his eighteenth birthday:

dance battles,
gang fights,
block parties.

But he dreamed of making a movie.

SCRIPT IDEA:
BOY: Mickey. No game. No girls. Meets
GIRL: Jesse, the young girlfriend of
BOY: Mickey's landlord.
GIRL: Jesse teaches
BOY: Mickey everything he needs to know about
GIRL: How to impress them. How to treat them. But
BOY: Mickey uses what he learns to get
GIRL: Jesse to fall in love with him, but her
    boyfriend,
BOY: Mickey's landlord, finds out and kicks him and
GIRL: Jesse out of the building.
    So they're in love,
    but they're homeless,
    but they're happy.
Right.

CASTING OF THE WORST, STUPIDEST MOVIE EVER

BOY: Mickey
   to be played by Uncle Mark's little brother,
   my father,
   Mikey.

GIRL: Jesse
   to be played by the younger sister of a girl
   Uncle Mark used to date,
   Shari,
   my mother.

UNCLE MARK PULLED ME IN

for a hug,
but how you
hug what's haunting you?

AND YOU KNOW

it's weird to know
a person you don't know

and at the same time

not know
a person you know,

you know?

09:08:25 a.m.

WHY YOU HERE?

I asked Uncle Mark,

taking my turn,
my time,
looking him up
and down.

Sadness
split his face
like cold breeze
on chapped lip
after attempting
to smile.

I guess he expected me
to be excited to see him.
And I was, sorta,

but still.

WITH HIS HAND

he brushed down the front
of his shirt,
smoothing out wrinkles,
straightening himself out.

Pants stopped
just at the top of his
dress shoes,
dress shoes tied
in perfect bows,
leather shiny,
uncreased
like he ain't
been walking.

Brushed and brushed
down his chest
to stomach,
down his thighs,

then squatting,
dipped a finger in
his mouth and scrubbed
the toe of his shoe,
a smudge
not there.

A BETTER QUESTION,

he said,
eyes up at me

is, why are you here?

RANDOM THOUGHT NO. 2

Always
always
always

be skeptical of a person
who answers a question
by asking a question.

Usually
usually
usually

it's a setup.

ANAGRAM NO. 3

COOL = LOCO

WHAT YOU MEAN?

I asked,
trying to avoid
having to talk about
the coldness
in my heart
and the heater
in my waist.

WHAT DO I MEAN?

He stood up.

> *What do I mean?*

he repeated,
putting
hands together,
fingertips touching,
cracking what sounded
like all the knuckles
in the world.

> *Listen, kid,*
> *don't play me and*
> *don't play with me.*
> *It's best you*
> *turn it loose before*
> *I tighten you up.*

OKAY, OKAY,

I begged,
trying to hold him off,
trying to avoid being
knotted up again.

Look,
they killed Shawn
last night, Uncle Mark.
And . . .

And today
you woke up ready
to make things
right, right?

I nodded.

And the reason why
is because for the
first time in your life,
you realise, or at least
you think you could
kill someone,
right?

I nodded.

RIGHT?

he said,
louder.

Right.

BUT TO EXPLAIN MYSELF

I said,

*The Rules are
the rules.*

UNCLE MARK HUFFED

closed his eyes.

I wondered if he
was thinking

about The Rules.

He knew them
like I knew them.

Passed to him.
Passed them to his little brother.
Passed to my older brother.
Passed to me.

The Rules
have always ruled.

Past present future forever.

UNCLE MARK SQUEEZED HIS LIPS

like he was trying
to rip them off.

Then opened
his eyes.

Okay, Will,

he said,
all serious.

Let's set the scene.

What you mean,
set the scene?

*I mean, let's play it out,
how this whole thing is gon'
go down. Play it out
like a movie,*

Uncle Mark explained.

*We'll go back and forth.
I'll start, from the top.*

THE SCENE

Will stands over dead brother, Shawn.
Two holes in his chest. Blood all over the
ground.

Will takes his mother inside.
She cries. He looks for his brother's
gun.

Will finds the gun. Lies down and thinks
about The Rules. No crying. No snitching.
And always get revenge.

The next day, he decides to find
who he knows killed his brother.
A guy named Riggs.

Will gets in the elevator. Goes down to the
lobby. Walks outside, past his brother's
blood on the concrete.

He continues for nine blocks,
gets to Riggs's house, sees Riggs,
pulls the gun out and . . .

I GOT STUCK

Couldn't say
nothing else. Couldn't say
it. Hoped Uncle Mark would say,

cut.

BUT HE DIDN'T (the scene, continued)

Go 'head. Finish it.

Up until that point
things were running
smoothly, but this
stupid last part
got me caught up.

Finish it!

Uncle Mark demanded.
Dani whimpered.
Buck razzed.

Okay, okay,

I said,
trying to calm
Uncle Mark down.

*Will pulls the gun out,
and . . .*

I stalled.

And . . . and . . .

MY MOUTH

dried out,
words phlegm
trapped in my throat,
like an allergic reaction
to the thought
of it all.

THE SCENE (completed)

And . . .

                And shoots.

Uncle Mark
finished it for me,
said it slowly,
dragging out the
shhhhhhhhhhhh.

Then I could
finally
painfully
hack it up.

And shoots.

FOR THE RECORD,

this movie

would've been better
than that stupid one
he was trying to make
when he was alive

that's for sure.

Maybe not as happy.
But definitely better.

STORY NO. 2 ABOUT UNCLE MARK

Uncle Mark lost the camera
his mother got him,
the one he recorded
dance battles
and gang fights
and block parties
and the beginning of his
corny-ass movie on.

Couldn't afford another one.
OPTIONS:
    Could've asked Grandma again,
        but that would've been pointless.
    Could've stolen one,
        but he wasn't 'bout to be sweating,
        so he wasn't 'bout to be running.
    Could've gotten a job,
        but working was another one of those things
        Uncle Mark just wasn't 'bout to be doing.

So he did
what a lot of people do

around here.

HIS PLAN

To sell for one day.
One day.

Uncle Mark
took a corner,
pockets full
of rocks to
become rolls,
future finance,

and in an hour
had enough
money to buy
a new camera.

But decided
to stick at it

just through
the end of the day.
That's all.

Just through
the end
of
the
day.

I'M SURE

you

know

where

this

is

going.

HE HELD THAT CORNER

for a day,
for a week,
for a month,

full-out
pusher,
money-making
pretty boy,

a target
for a ruthless
young hustler
whose name

Mom can never
remember.

THAT GUY TOOK THE CORNER

from Uncle Mark.
Snatched it right from
under him.

And it wasn't peaceful.
Everybody
ran ducked hid tucked
themselves tight
blew their own eardrums
gouged their own eyes.

Did what they'd all
been trained to.

Pretended like yellow tape
was some kind of
neighbourhood flag
that don't nobody wave
but always be flapping
in the wind.

UNCLE MARK SHOULD'VE

just bought his camera
and shot his stupid movie
after the first day.

Unfortunately,
he never shot nothing
ever again.

But my father did.

ANAGRAM NO. 4

CINEMA = ICEMAN

RANDOM THOUGHT NO. 3

Not sure
what an iceman is,
but it makes me think
of bad dudes.

Cold-blooded.

09:08:31 a.m.

SO ANYWAY, AFTER I SAID IT,

and shoots,

it was like the words
came out and at the same
time went in.

Went down
into me and
chewed on everything
inside as if
I had somehow
swallowed
my own teeth
and they were
sharper than
I'd ever known.

MEANWHILE,

Uncle Mark
reached into his
shirt pocket,
pulled out two
cigarettes.

Great.
More smoke.

I hoped
the second one
wasn't for me.

I don't smoke.
Shit is gross.

Plus, people
who living,
who real,
                  like me
ain't allowed
to smoke
in elevators.

AND WHAT HAPPENS NEXT IN THIS MOVIE?

    Uncle Mark asked,
    tucking one cig
    behind his ear,
    booger-rolling the other
    between his fingers.

Nothing.
That's it. The end.

    I shrugged.

    He positioned the cig
    in the corner of his mouth,
    patted his pockets
    for fire.

        The end?

    he murmured,
    looking at Buck,
    motioning for a light.

It's never the end,

Uncle Mark said,
all chuckle, chuckle.
He leaned towards Buck.

Never.

Buck struck a match.

And the elevator came to a stop,
again.

THIS TIME

there was no smoke
blocking the door,
even though there were
three people—

I guess, people—

in the elevator,
smoking.

I know
it don't make sense,
but stay with me.

AND THERE HE WAS,

clear as day
as the door
slid open.

Recognised
him instantly.

Been waiting
for him since
I was three.

Mikey Holloman.

—

My father.

09:08:32 a.m.

MY POP

stepped in the elevator,
stood right in front of me,
stared

as if looking
at his own reflection,
as if he'd stepped into
a time machine.
Moments

later spread his arms,
welcomed me into
a lifetime's worth
of squeeze.

IS IT POSSIBLE

for a hug
to peel back skin
of time,
the toughened
and raw bits,
the irritated
and irritating
dry spots,

the parts that bleed?

POP PULLED AWAY,

noticed his brother,
gave Uncle Mark
a firm handshake,
yanked him in
for a half hug

just like on
all the pictures.

No sound in the
elevator except
hands popping
together and
the muted thud
of pats on backs.

I HAVE NO MEMORIES

of my father.
Shawn always tried to get me to
remember things like

> Pop dressing up as Michael Jackson
> for Halloween and, after trick-or-treating,
> riding us up and down in this elevator,
> doing his best moonwalk but
> not enough space to go nowhere,
> slamming into walls.

Shawn swore I laughed
so hard I farted,
stunk up the whole elevator,
even peed myself.

I was only three.
And I don't remember that.
I've always wanted to,

but I don't.

> I *so* don't.

A BROKEN HEART

killed my dad.
That's what my mother
always said.

And as a kid
I always figured
his heart
was forreal broken
like an arm
or a toy

or the middle drawer.

BUT THAT'S NOT WHAT SHAWN SAID.

Shawn always said
our dad was killed
for killing the man
who killed our uncle.

Said he was at a pay
phone, probably talking
to Mom, when a guy
walked up on him,

put pistol to head,
asked him if he knew a
guy who went by Gee.
Don't know what Pop said.

But that was the end
of that story.

I ALWAYS USED TO ASK

Shawn how he knew that.
Especially the whole
Gee thing.

He said
Buck told him.
Said that was
Buck's corner.

It was then that Buck
started looking out
for Shawn, who at
the time
was only seven.

Buck was sixteen.

But I don't remember
none of this

either.

HI, WILL.

My father's voice
brand-new to me.

Deep.
Some scratch
on the tail of each word.

How I figured
Shawn's would've
sounded

someday.

HOW YOU BEEN?

Weird talking to my dad
like he was a stranger
even though we hugged
like family.

A'ight, I guess,

I said,
unsure of what else to say.

How do you small-talk your father
when "dad" is a language so foreign
that whenever you try to say it,
it feels like you got a third lip
and a second tongue?

I WANTED TO UNLOAD,

just tell him
about Shawn,
and how Mom
cried and drank
and scratched
herself to sleep,
how I was feeling,
The Rules,
all that.

Wanted to
tell him everything
in that stuffy elevator,
but I held back
because

Buck,
Dani and
Uncle Mark
were watching
with warm,
weird faces.

I ALREADY KNOW,

Pop said,
taking a
deep breath.

I know,
I know,
I know.

Sadness
and love
in his voice.

I replied,
choking down me
choking up,

I don't know,
I don't know,
I don't know

what to do.

I WIPED MY FACE

with the back of my hand,
knuckles rolling over my eyes
to catch water before it
came down.

No crying.

Not in front of Pop.
Not in front of Dani.
Not in front of none

of these people.

Not in front of no one.
Never.

WHAT YOU THINK YOU SHOULD DO?

he asked.

Follow The Rules,

I said
just like I told
everybody else.

Just like you did.

POP GAVE UNCLE MARK

a look when Uncle Mark
asked if I had ever heard
my father's story.

Of course,

I said.

*He was killed
at a pay phone.*

Worry washed
over Pop's face.
Opened his
mouth to speak
but changed
his mind,
then changed
his mind
again.

*That's not the story
we talking about.
What you know
is how I was killed,*

Pop explained.

*But you don't know ...
You just don't know ...*

WHEN MARK WAS SHOT

I was shattered. Shifted.
Never the same again.
Like shards of my own heart
shivving me on the inside,
just like your mama told you.

You and Shawn were little
and I couldn't just come home
and be a daddy and a husband
when I couldn't be a brother
no more.

Not after what happened.
And how it happened.

But I didn't cry. Didn't snitch.
Knew exactly who killed Mark.
Knew I could get him.

The Rules.

Taught to me
by Mark.
Taught to him
by our pop.

That night
I walked two blocks to where
Mark used to move,
where dirt was done.

And waited and waited
until finally a dude came
from a building,
stepped up to his corner
        Mark's corner
slapped a pack in
a customer's clutch.

Money was exchanged
and I knew that was my guy,
the guy that shot my brother
dead in the street.

I made my move.
Hood over my head.
Gun from my waist
and by the time he saw me
I was already squeezing.

POP! POP! POP!

By the third
he was down,
but I gave him one more
just because I was angry.

So angry.

Like something
had gotten into me.

THAT SOMETHING

that my pop said
had gotten into him

must be
what my mom
meant by

the night-time.

POP SAID

he took off running
so fast his sneakers
barely touched

concrete.

Said he took
the long way,
turned pistol into poof,
turned bang-bang into hush-hush.

WHEN I GOT HOME

I took a hot shower,
hot enough
to burn the skin
off my body,

      he said.

Couldn't kiss your mother,
couldn't kiss you boys
good night.
Just lay naked
in the scummy bathtub,
the cold porcelain
keeping me from sleep

from nightmares.

BUT YOU DID WHAT YOU HAD TO DO,

I said,
after listening to
my father admit
what I had already
known,

     The Rules
     are the rules.

UNCLE MARK AND MY FATHER

looked at me with hollow eyes
dancing somewhere between
guilt and grief,
which I couldn't make sense of
until my father admitted

that he had killed

the wrong guy.

YOU AIN'T KILL GEE?

I asked,
confused.

No, I did,

Pop confirmed,
his voice crumbling.

But Gee didn't kill Mark.
Gee was just some young kid
trying to be tough,
trying make
a few friends,
a few bucks,
a flunky
for the guy who
killed Mark,

he explained.

Then
Then why
Then why you
kill him?

I asked.

I didn't know
he wasn't the right guy,

Pop said,
a tremble in
his throat.

I was sure that was Mark's killer.

Had
to
be.

I LEANED

against the wall
next to Dani, thinking,
staring at my father who
wasn't my father at all.

At least not like I had imagined him.
A man who moved with precision,
patience, purpose,
not no willy-nilly
buck-bucking off
at randoms
at random.

Spent my whole damn life
missing a misser.
That disappointed me.

And he stood on the
other side of the elevator
staring back at me,
wasn't sure what he
was thinking.

Maybe that I was exactly how he had imagined.
Maybe that disappointed him.

RANDOM THOUGHT NO. 4

There's this thing I used to see
kids at the playground do
with their dads.

They'd stand on their father's feet,

the dads holding the
kids by the arms, walking
stiff-legged like zombies.

The kids had to trust the fathers
to guide them because the fathers
could see what was coming

but the kids,
holding tight to their dads,
moved blindly

backwards.

THEN POP MADE THE FIRST MOVE.

A step forwards.
I made the next.
Then he took another.
We met in the middle.

Again,

dove into each other.
This time the hug,
a mix of I miss you
and who are you
and I'm confused
and I'm cracking
and I don't know what
the hell to do
or where the hell to go.

My father's hand
gripped my back
as I did my best
to bury myself
in his armpit,

to get lost in the new
and strangely familiar feeling

of fatherhood.

AND THAT'S WHEN IT HAPPENED.

He pulled the gun
from my waistband.

And put it to my head.

I FREAKED OUT.

What you doin'?

> I shrilled,
> in shock.

What the hell you doin'!

> Eye-to-eye,
> a tear streaming
> down his face.

> Just one,
> so it ain't
> really count.

> Chest aching
> like a weight
> crushing me,
> biscuit tight
> against my temple.

> He cocked it.
> Sounded like
> a door closing.

I CALLED OUT

for help
but couldn't
see no one.

Not Uncle Mark,
or Dani,
or Buck,
or hear them,
or even smell
the dank
of tobacco turning to tar.

Like it was suddenly
just the two of us,
me and my dad,
both of us apparently
losing
our minds.

POP STOOD OVER ME,

the gun pressed against
the side of my face.

Was the first time I had
ever had one to my head.
First time I had been that
close to death. To the end.

And at the hand of
Pop. Pop? Pop!

YOU WOULD THINK

I would be thinking
about whether or not
he could actually do it
since he wasn't real.

But the hugs were real.
And the gun was real.

Weren't no ghost bullets
in that clip.

Those were real bullets.

Fifteen total.
One for every year
of my life.

MY STOMACH

was aching,
the quaking world
in the bottom of it,
and it wasn't long
before I could feel

myself splitting
apart.

A WARM SENSATION

ran through the lower
half of my body,
seeping
down my leg
into my sneakers.

Cigarette smoke
cut once again,
this time by the smell
of my own piss.

09:08:40 a.m.

THEN POP UNCOCKED THE GUN,

wrapped his arms around me
again,

squeezed tight like
I was some rag doll,
stuffed

the gun back into
my waistband.

THEY TOO UNLOCKED THE SUN,

I SCREAMED,

pushed him away,
yelled until my throat
stripped,
until my words became
sizzle.

Weak.
Wet.
Worried
about looking like
a punk-ass kid.

And my father
leaned against the wall,
staring,
chin up,
cocky,
quiet,

while I exploded.

AND LIKE OLD TIMES

Uncle Mark
came to his side
like a brother,

pulled the extra cig,
the one tucked
behind his ear,

handed it to
my father,
chest heaving.

Eyes on me,
he threw the cig
in his mouth.

Buck took his cue.
I backed into
a corner,

wished this
stupid elevator
would get to *L*,

for this whole
thing to hurry up
and be done.

                    Buck struck
                    a match and the
                    elevator came

                    to a stop.

3

A STRANGER,

chubby,
light skin,
almost white,
the type that
turns red,
that burns,
dirty brown hair
curled up
on his head,

got in the elevator
like a normal guy.

Didn't acknowledge
nobody.

No dead body.
No live body.
No smoke.

Normal.

SO I FIGURED

he was real.

Which
made me real

embarrassed
about the pee

but
made me real

happy
I wasn't all

the way gone.

THE THICK PALE DUDE

stood staring at his
blurry reflection in
the metal door

when Buck started
trying to get his
attention.

Yo,

Buck said.

Psst.

The guy didn't
budge.

Yo, dude,

Buck called,
reaching
for his
shoulder.

THE MAN TURNED AROUND.

I know you.

Buck flashed his
big choppy grin.

Your name
Frick, right?

Only to people who
know me
know me,

the guy said,
reluctantly reaching
for Buck's hand.

Remember me?

Buck said,
like a distant
relative at a
reunion.

Buck,

he said,
showing the back
of his T-shirt again.

> *Oh shit,*
> *Buck?*

Head cocked.

> *Buck?*

Arms wide.

> *What's good, man?*

Nothing.
Is good.
At all.

THIS IS

Dani,
Mark,
Mikey
and

you remember
Shawn?

This his little brother,

Will.

BEFORE FRICK COULD ANSWER,

I asked Buck
how he knew
him,

what his connection
was to me,

what he was doing
in this spooky-ass

elevator.

09:08:50 a.m.

HOW DO I KNOW HIM?

**Buck scoffed,
shaking his head.**

*This is the man
who murdered me.*

WAIT.

Wait.

Wait . . . wait.

Hold up.

Hold

up.

Hold the hell

on.

On my brother,

on Shawn's name,

You serious?

Wait . . .
Wha?

Wait, wait, wait.

. . .

What?

YOU HEARD ME RIGHT.

See, Frick here—

Buck paused.

Why they call you that, anyway?

he asked,
sidetracked.

It's really Frank. Twin sister,
Francis. Frick and Frack
came from my uncle.
Stupid shit old men call you
stick in the hood,

Frick explained.

Who you tellin'.
Matter fact because
of you—

Buck paused again,
turned back to me.

Because
of him, Will,

the only reason
people 'round here
know my government name
is from reading it on
my damn tombstone.

BUCK'S REAL NAME

was James.

I've only heard it one time.

Buck better
than James.

Buck short
for young-buck.

Nickname given
by stepfather as a joke

because Buck
couldn't grow no facial hair.

Smooth baby face,
nothing rough

about it.

BUCK WAS TWO-SIDED.

Two dads,
step and real.

Step raised him:
      a preacher,
      a real preacher,
      not scared of no one,
      praying for anyone,
      helping everyone.

Real run through him:
      a bank robber,
      would steal air from the world
      if he could get his hands on it.

PEOPLE ALWAYS SAID

he was taught to do good
but doing bad
was in his blood.

And there's that night-time
Mom always be talking about.

It'll snatch your teaching
from you,

put a gun in your hand,
a grumble in your gut,
and some sharp in your teeth.

BUT HE DIDN'T START THAT WAY.

At first Buck was
a small-time hustler,
dime bags on the corner.

Same old story
until my pop got popped
at the pay phone that night.

Then he became a big brother
to Shawn
and a robber to a bunch of
suburban neighbourhoods
every morning
            (he knew better than to
            jack people around here)

and come back with
money (the most)
sneakers (the best)
and jewellery (which he loved to show off).

BACK TO FRICK.

I was shocked
when I heard that
this dude killed Buck.

                    Yeah,

Buck said,
hand on
Frick's shoulder
all buddy-buddy.

                    This the guy.

He glanced
at me.

                    *Shawn never
                    told you that story?*

HE NEVER REALLY TALKED ABOUT IT,

I said.

*Shawn just said
you were shot
and that he knew
who did it,*

I explained,
remembering that time.
Shawn's face a candle,
melted wax,
flame flickering out.

I remember the cops
banging on our door
to question him,

to tell him they heard
he was close to James—

that was the one time
I heard Buck's real name—

and to ask him
if he knew who might've

done it,
killed him,
shot him
twice

in the stomach,
in the street.

SHAWN AIN'T SAY NOTHING

to the cops,
to no one,

just locked
himself

in his room
for hours

and the next
day I caught him

sitting on his
bed pushing

bullets into
gun clip.

09:08:54 a.m.

WELL, LET ME TELL YOU,

Buck said.

*We were hanging out at the court
sharing a bottle of something cheap
and strong just before it went down,*

Buck said.

*Shawn was telling me how he had
gotten into a little scuffle, nothing
major, with one of the dudes from
the Dark Suns,*

Buck said.

*Said he had to get your mother
some kind of soap she uses that
he could only get from the store
down by where they hang out.*

A DUMB THING TO SAY

would've been to
tell Buck how important
that soap was

that it stopped Mom from
scraping loose a river
of wounds.

But instead
I just said,

Riggs.

I'M NOT SURE WHAT HIS NAME IS,

Buck said.

Said Shawn
said he was
going to the
store when
the dude   *Riggs*
ran up on
him talking
all this shit.

Said it was
nothing
serious, just
poppin' off
at the mouth
about how he
was a Dark Sun
and how Shawn
ain't belong
around there.

Said Shawn
was in his
feelings
all huff-huff
explaining to
Buck how he
had grown up
with the kid   *Riggs*
and how the
kid was brand-new.

Buck said
he told Shawn
to let it roll off,
but he couldn't
because that's
just how he was.

All emotional
all the time,

Buck said.

WHILE HE'S GOING ON ABOUT THIS DUDE,

I'm trying to show him this chain
I just got from some kid out in
the burbs. Didn't even snatch it.
I just growled a little bit and asked
for it and the sucka just took it
right off and handed it to me.
Ain't even snatch it,

> Buck said,
> thinking back on that day
> like he still couldn't
> believe it.

> > *But what does that have to with*
> > *my brother and this guy?*

> I said,
> pointing to Frick.

Hold on.
I'm gettin' to that.

SO BECAUSE SHAWN WAS

tripping so hard about this dude,
I gave him the gold chain,

      Buck said,
      proud.

A gift.
His first one.
Then Shawn left
the basketball court.

            And that's when I came,

      Frick chimed in,
      a big smile
      on his face
      like he had just
      won some
      kind of award.

HOW TO BECOME A DARK SUN

1. TURF:
>   nine blocks from where I live.

2. THE SHINING:
>   a cigarette burn under the right eye.

3. DARK DEED:
>   robbing someone,
>   beating someone

>   or the worst,
>   killing someone.

Note: Apparently, you also gotta be corny.

I WAS ASSIGNED

> my Dark Deed
> for initiation,

Frick explained.

And it was to kill Buck?

> *No,*

he said.

> *Funny thing is,*
> *I was just supposed*
> *to rob him.*

I didn't think it was
a *funny thing* at all.

> *Everybody knew*
> *Buck was always flossin',*
> *always flashy. But nobody*
> *would touch him because*
> *of his pops. Both of them.*

> *Real and step.*

GANGSTAS

always respect
older
        (original)
gangstas
        (OGs)
and preachers
who act like

gangstas.

FRICK SAID

his plan was to
jack the jack-boy.

Said he knew Buck
would be at the court

so he ran up on him,
pulled the hammer,

and got laughed at.

BUCK SAID

he couldn't get got
by a dude who he could
tell was as soft as the
suburban joker he'd
just jacked.

Everybody in the
elevator laughed.

Except for me.

09:08:58 a.m.

WHATEVER, MAN

       Frick said.

I was just trying to
earn my stripes.

Can't knock me for that.

       He turned around,
       caught eyes with
       Pop and Uncle Mark.
       They nodded in agreement.

              No judgment over here,

       Uncle Mark said,
       throwing his hands up.

Anyway, this crazy fool,
Buck, swings at me.
Just tries to take me
even though I had a boom stick!

       Frick looked
       at Buck, shook
       his head, then cut
       his eyes to me.

I got scared.

So I pulled
the trigger.

BUCK BENT

his pinky and ring
finger back,
turned his
hand into
a gun.

Bang-
bang.

AGAIN

What does this have to do
with Shawn?

       I asked.

               Shawn stuck to The Rules,

       Frick replied.

You mean . . .

       I swallowed.

You mean he . . . he . . .

       I struggled
       to get it out.

       Now Buck put
       the finger gun
       against Frick's
       chest and repeated,

Bang-bang.

ACTUALLY

he only pulled the
trigger once, so it
was more like,
Bang,

Frick corrected.

Fifteen
bullets.

TOOK ME OUT

before I ever even
got my Shining,

    Frick said.

    Rubbed just under
    his right eye
    like it still
    rubbed him
    the wrong way.

FRICK YANKED HIS COLLAR DOWN.

See this?

he asked,
exposing a hole
in his chest,
dime-sized,
disgusting,
bloody
but not
bleeding.

*Your brother's
fingerprints are in
there somewhere.*

Buck *Ha*'d!
and replied
before I had
a chance.

*And I bet
it's his
middle finger!*

WHEN THE JOKE WAS OVER

I asked how Shawn
could've known Frick
was the guy who killed Buck.

Buck said there was only
one other person at the
court that night,
always there
all the time,

a young kid
running back and forth
trying to dunk.
Not shoot.

Said he thinks
I might've known him.

Tony.

And he wasn't trying to dunk.
He was trying to
                    fly.

TONY TALKING

ain't the same as snitching.

Snitching is bumping gums
to badges, but
Tony ain't run to no cops
or cry to no cameras,
nothing like that.

Tony talking
was laying claim,
loyalty,
an allegiance to
the asphalt around
here, an attempt
to grow taller
            get bigger
one way or another.

09:09:03 a.m.

NOW LET ME ASK YOU

how you know
this kid Riggs got your brother?

Buck fired back.

Because he clearly got revenge
for Shawn taking out this guy,

I pointed
to Frick.

Frick, you know
a kid named Riggs?

Dani asked
out of nowhere,
her voice
floating over
my shoulder.

Little dude.
Big mouth.
Dark Sun.

I figured
the description
might help.

Frick looked at me,
confused.

Who?

ANAGRAM NO. 6

**I wish I knew
an anagram**

for POSER.

FRICK LOOKED

at me like I was crazy,
shrugged his shoulders,
and turned around
and faced the door.

I couldn't see
his reflection.

I couldn't see
any of their
reflections.

Just mine,
blurred.

FRICK HAD

his own cigarettes
and
his own matches.

Finally
Finally
Finally

the elevator came to a stop.

WHEN THE ELEVATOR DOOR OPENED

no one was there.
I reached over and pushed
the *L* button
again and again and
again and again.

Because that's what you do
when you want the door
to close faster.

Another one of those
elevator rules.

COME ON,

I huffed
under my breath,

impatient,
pissy,
pissed off,
scared,
scarred,
and straight up
uncomfortable being
crammed in this
stupid
steel
box,

this vertical coffin,

another second.

UNCLE MARK CHUCKLED.

*You would never survive
in prison, nephew.*

FINALLY

the elevator door
began closing.

I exhaled,
happy we were
almost there.

One floor to go.

And just before
it was shut,
before the door clicked
in place,
four fingers slipped in
just barely catching it.

The elevator door
began opening

again.

09:09:07 a.m.

HIM.

Shawn.

**Stepped into the smoky box
wearing exactly what he wore
the night before:**
> **blue jeans,**
> **T-shirt,**
> **gold chain.**

**But not his alive outfit.
His dead one.**

**The one that came
with bloodstains.**

EVERYBODY

was so happy
to see him.

Shawn!

Buck yelped,
reaching out
for him.

They slapped hands.
Buck fiddled with
the gold chain around
Shawn's neck.
Moved the clasp
to the back.

Shawn looked at Dani.

Look at you!

he said,
taking her hand,
spinning her around.

Uncle Mark
gave him a light
tap in the ribs.

Big man!

> he said
> proudly.

> Shawn turned,
> gave him a hug,
> caught a glimpse
> of our father.

>   *Pop!*

> he said,
> natural,
> his face
> beaming.

> Our father
> wrapped his arms
> around Shawn,
> cocooning him.

> Then pulled away,
> shook hands
> like men,

> like partners.

ALL

the un-alive/un-dead
lined up along the wall
puffing their cigs,
smiling

as Shawn
finally
            finally
faced
me.

WHEN WE WERE KIDS

I would follow Shawn
around the apartment
making the strangest
noise with my mouth.

Hard to explain the sound.
Burpy but not a burp.

Like burp mixed
with yawn mixed
with hum.

Something like that.

For twenty minutes straight.
From bedroom
to kitchen
to living room
back to bedroom.

To punish me,
he would wait for me to finish,
to run out of steam,
to let it go,
to get tired

of being immature.

And then,
to my surprise,
he wouldn't say a word to me
for the rest
of the day.

I LOOKED AT SHAWN.

He looked at me.

Shawn,

I said.

But he said
nothing.

I repeated,

Shawn?

Nothing.

I STEPPED TOWARDS HIM,

hugged him.
He didn't hug back.

Just stood there,
awkward,

a middle drawer
of a man.

I ASKED HIM

why he wouldn't say nothing,
why he was ignoring me,

but still,
nothing,
not a word,

not even a smile.

I TOLD HIM

about the
drawer,
the gun,

that I did
like he told me,
like Buck told him,
like our grandfather told
our uncle, like our uncle
told our dad.

I followed The Rules.
At least the first two.

I hadn't cried.
I hadn't snitched.

EXPLAINED

that I was on my way to take
care of his killer,

follow through
with Rule Number Three.

Told him I knew it was Riggs.
Told him I thought it was Riggs,
then told him I knew it was Riggs
again.

CONFESSED

that I was scared,
that I needed
to know I was
doing the right thing.

THE RULES ARE THE RULES

Right? Right? Right?
Right? Right? Right? Right? Right?
Right?   Right?
Right?   Right?
Right?   Right?
Right?   Right?
Right?   Right?
Right?   Right?
Right?   Right?
Right?   Right?
Right?   Right?
Right?   Right?
                                Right?
                               Right?
                              Right?
                             Right?
                            Right?
                           Right?
                          Right?
                         Right?
                        Right?
                       Right?
                      Right?
                     Right?
                    Right?
                   Right?
                  Right?
                 Right?

Shawn?

I WAS BREAKING DOWN.

The tears were coming
and I did what I could
to hold them back.

Took my eyes off Shawn,
hoping to fight the crying
feeling by not looking.

But everywhere else
was everyone else,
cigarettes glowing

like a bunch of
L buttons.

09:09:08 a.m.

I LOOKED BACK AT SHAWN,

tears now pouring from his eyes
as he softly snotted and hiccupped
like a little kid,

tears pouring from his eyes
tears pouring from his eyes
tears   pouring   from   his   eyes.

I thought you said
no crying,
Shawn,

I said,
voice cracking,
one of my tears
bursting
free.

But only one
so it didn't count.

No crying.

No crying.
No crying.
No crying.

AND EVEN THOUGH

his face was wet
with tears he wasn't
supposed to cry
when he was alive

I couldn't see him
as anything less
than my brother,

my favourite,
my only.

AND THERE WAS A SOUND

like whatever makes
elevators work,

cables and cogs,
or whatever,

grinding,
rubbing metal on metal

like a machine moaning
but coming

from the mouth
from the belly

of Shawn.
He never said nothing to me.

Just made that painful
piercing sound,

as suddenly the
elevator came to a stop.

RANDOM THOUGHT NO. 5

The sound you hear
in your head,

the one people call
ears ringing,

sounds less like a bell,
and more like a flatline.

THERE WAS A MOMENT

before the door opened
when we all just stood there,
sickening
smoke thickening,

crowded in

this cell
this coffin
this elevator

quiet.

I LOOKED AROUND

only seeing the orange glow

of five cigarettes puncturing
the sheet of smoke
like headlights in a
heavy fog.

Only five cigarettes.

Shawn hadn't lit one,
became invisible
in the cloud.

And I felt like
the cigarette meant for him
was burning in
my stomach,

filling me with
stinging fire.

09:09:09 a.m.

I WANT OUT.

The door opened slowly,
the cloud of smoke
rushing out of the elevator,
rushing out of me
like an angry wave.

I caught my breath as

Buck,
Dani,
Uncle Mark,
Pop,
Frick
and
Shawn

chased behind it.

The *L* button
no longer lit.

I stood alone
in the empty box,
face tight from
dried tears,
jeans soggy,
a loaded gun
still tucked in my
waistband.

Shawn
turned back towards me,
eyes dull from death
but shining from tears,

finally spoke
to me.

Just two words,
like a joke he'd
been saving.

YOU COMING?

Acknowledgments

I'd like to give special thanks to my agent, Elena Giovinazzo, who saw this work first and suggested I write it in verse; and to Larissa Helena, Alice Swan and all the great folks at Faber and Faber who took it, brought on the incredible Chris Priestley and helped me shape it into what it is now. Thank you. To my family, but more importantly, for this book, my friends, who have been with me in precarious situations where our humanity curdles and our ethics are put to the test. I couldn't have written this without our childhoods. To the young men and women serving time in detention facilities, your stories, your testimonies matter. Your lives are often sacrificed by the failures of people twice your age. But you will make it. You will make it. Also, to the poets. Without poetry, especially when I was younger, being a writer would've seemed like a futile attempt. The poets taught me the functionality and power of language. And lastly, to my dear friend, Randell Duncan. We miss you. Rest easy, brother.